The Rescue Princesses
The Golden Shell

Paula Harrison

nosy
crow

In memory of Alf and Dorothy

First published in the UK in 2014 by Nosy Crow Ltd
The Crow's Nest, 10a Lant Street
London, SE1 1QR, UK

Nosy Crow and associated logos are trademarks and/or registered
trademarks of Nosy Crow Ltd

Text © Paula Harrison, 2014
Cover illustration © Sharon Tancredi, 2014
Interior illustrations © Artful Doodlers, 2014

The right of Paula Harrison to be identified as the author of this work
has been asserted by her in accordance with the Copyright, Designs
and Patents Act, 1988

1 3 5 7 9 10 8 6 4 2

A CIP catalogue record for this book is available from the British Library

Printed and bound in the UK by Clays Ltd, St Ives Plc

Papers used by Nosy Crow are made from wood grown in
sustainable forests.

ISBN: 978 0 85763 343 9

www.nosycrow.com

First Day at School

Princess Ella gazed out at the trees and hedges flashing past the car window. She linked her fingers together tightly and tried to ignore the fluttering feeling in her tummy. It wouldn't be long now. Soon they would reach the Royal Academy for Princesses, her new school!

Ella tucked her dark, wavy hair behind her tiara and smoothed the grey pleats of her new school skirt. She was trying not to think about missing home, especially

1

her puppy, Sesame with his beautiful brown eyes and soft little paws. But thinking about her new school didn't make her feel better either. Her mum had told her that the school was enormous. What if she got lost trying to find her way around? What if none of the other girls wanted to talk to her? What if—

"Are you all right, Ella?" Her mum, Queen Jade, leaned towards her. "You look a little pale? Do you feel ill?"

"No, I'm fine." Ella tried to smile.

"Really?" The queen frowned. "You don't look fine. Perhaps we'd better stop for a moment." She leaned forward to speak to the royal driver. "Stop at the side of the road, please."

The car pulled over next to a hedge. Ella's dad, King George, gave a quiet snore from the front passenger seat.

"Your father's nodded off again," said

the queen, opening the car door. "Out you go! You'll feel much better after some fresh air."

Ella climbed out on to a grassy verge dotted with purple flowers. They were in a narrow lane with tall hedges on both sides. The sun shone brightly and thin wisps of white cloud floated in the sky.

The queen climbed out of the car, keeping hold of her golden crown. "Ah, there's something wonderful about the air here!" she said, smiling. "It makes me feel quite energetic! I remember when I used to come to school here, many years ago. One day we all went on a long walk through the fields and..." The queen carried on talking but Ella didn't listen closely to the rest.

Her mum had been talking about the old days at school quite a lot. She'd talked about it while making Ella try on her new green and grey uniform. Then she'd talked some more while packing Ella's suitcase. Ella knew that her mum had loved going to the Royal Academy for Princesses. She just wasn't sure she was going to like it, too!

She breathed in deeply. Her mum was right. The air did seem fresher here. She noticed a gap in the hedge a little further along and went to look through it. Sheep were grazing in the field on the other side. Ella stared at the view beyond the field and her heart beat faster. In the distance there was a towering red-stone castle and the sparkling blue sea.

"Wow! That's a really big castle." Ella gazed at its tall square turrets. It looked much more old-fashioned than their palace back home.

"There it is!" said her mum, joining her. "Harebell Castle – home to the Royal

Academy for Princesses."

"That's Harebell Castle? I didn't know we were so close!" said Ella, surprised.

"Yes, we're nearly there." The queen smiled. "Let's carry on. We should reach the school in a few minutes."

Ella glanced at Harebell Castle one more time before returning to the car. She still felt a little nervous but now she'd seen the castle she wanted to know what it was like inside.

They drove through the castle gates ten minutes later. As the car swept along, Ella stared at the large statues beside the driveway that had been clipped from privet hedges. One was a boat with a tall mast next to the shape of a sailor looking through a telescope. Ella's favourite was a tall starfish standing up on two legs.

A tall grey-haired lady was waiting for

them at the front entrance. She greeted them as they got out of the car and shook their hands.

"Good afternoon," she said in a clear and calm voice. "I'm Miss Goldwin, the Headmistress of the Royal Academy for Princesses, and you must be Princess Petronella."

Ella winced. Petronella was her full name but her mum and dad only used it when they were telling her off. "Could you call me Ella?" she said hopefully.

Miss Goldwin nodded. "Very well, Princess Ella! I hope you all had a good journey. Please come in." She led them through a door with sea creatures carved into the wood. Ella traced a finger along the carving of a long octopus's tentacle.

The red stone walls gave a warm feeling to the inside of the castle. Two long staircases rose upwards at opposite

ends of the hallway and met on a wide
balcony. In the centre of the balcony was
a huge bronze-coloured bell standing on
a wooden pedestal.

Queen Jade looked around, beaming.
"It's just like I remember – the pictures
of famous pupils on the walls and the
smell of chocolate pudding. I had such a
wonderful time here."

Miss Goldwin led them into a large hall
set out with tables. "This is our dining
hall. We have assemblies in here on a
Friday and put on concerts and plays
at the end of term." She swept a speck
of dust off a nearby table. "Term began
two weeks ago. You'll be sharing a room
with three other girls who have also just
started here."

A girl with short blonde hair came in.
"Did you want to see me, Miss Goldwin?"
she asked with a curtsy.

"Yes, I did, Rosalind," replied the head teacher. "This is Ella, who will be taking the empty bunk bed in your room. Please would you show her where she'll be sleeping?"

Rosalind nodded. "Yes, Miss Goldwin, and then maybe I should show her around the rest of the school."

"An excellent idea!" Miss Goldwin turned to Ella. "Rosalind will be your guide today and I'll get someone to bring your suitcase upstairs in a moment."

"Goodbye, darling." Queen Jade hugged Ella. "Have a lovely time. We'll send you postcards from everywhere we go on our royal tour."

"Bye, Mum. Bye, Dad." Ella hugged them both. "I'll see you soon!" She felt excitement fizzing inside her as she followed Rosalind out of the hall.

"Have you had a really long journey?" asked Rosalind.

"Yes, it took five days to sail here from the Island of Varras. I like being on the ocean though." Ella stopped, suddenly shy.

Rosalind smiled. "Come on – I'll show you where we sleep!"

Ella hurried after her. She couldn't wait to see her new bunk bed and look all around the rest of the castle!

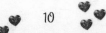

Chapter Two

Seahorse Tower

Ella followed Rosalind across the entrance hall and up the grand staircase. "Are you new here too?"

Rosalind nodded. "I started two weeks ago, at the beginning of term. So did Lottie and Summer, the other girls in our room. We wondered who would come to take the last bunk bed."

"I should have arrived at the start of term like you," explained Ella. "But my mum and dad couldn't bring me till now

 11

because they've been getting ready for their royal tour. They'll be visiting places for weeks and weeks."

The girls reached the balcony and Ella stared at the enormous bronze-coloured bell.

"They ring the bell three times for each mealtime," said Rosalind, noticing where Ella was looking.

"A bell that big must be really loud," said Ella.

"It is!" Rosalind turned a corner and led them up another staircase. "The castle has four towers and that's where we sleep. We're in Seahorse Tower."

Ella noticed three more staircases leading off in different directions. "What are the other towers called?" she asked.

"As well as Seahorse there's Coral, Jellyfish and Barnacle," Rosalind told her. "I wouldn't want to sleep in Barnacle.

Their tower always seems so cold. Anyway, here we are!"

She pushed open a door that was painted with a gigantic picture of a seahorse and decorated with shells. The corridor beyond was painted bluey-green with wavy shapes along it. Ella almost felt as if she was underwater.

The bedroom was large with bunk beds at both ends and plenty of cupboards. Two girls were perched together on a top bunk with their legs hanging over the edge. They were both wearing the Academy uniform and pretty tiaras. They looked up as Ella walked in.

A girl with curly red hair and sparkling green eyes jumped down from the bunk. "Hello, I'm Lottie! Are you the new girl?"

Ella smiled. "Yes, I'm Ella!"

"I'm Summer." The second girl climbed down from the bunk and pushed her

  13

golden hair behind her ears. "I hope you don't mind having a bottom bunk. Lottie and I took the top ones when we arrived."

"No, I don't mind." Ella noticed the seahorse quilts on each of the beds. "Are there lots of bedrooms in Seahorse Tower?"

"Five," said Lottie. "It's the smallest tower but the cosiest one, too! We'll show you round the whole place. You have to see the stables. And you must see the music room, and the garden and the pet barn."

Ella's eyebrows rose. She was just about to ask what the pet barn was when Rosalind broke in. "It's *my* job to show her around, Lottie. Miss Goldwin asked me especially!"

Lottie folded her arms. "All right! Don't get your tentacles in a tangle! We can all show her round together, can't we?"

Ella liked that idea. She was just wondering how to agree with Lottie without upsetting Rosalind, when a brightly-coloured parrot flew in through the open window. The bird landed on Summer's shoulder, folded his blue wings and looked beadily at Ella. He tilted his head and gave a loud squawk.

"Shh, Kanga!" said Summer. "You're not supposed to be in here."

A door banged further up the corridor.

"Quick, Summer!" said Rosalind. "That could be Molly checking up on us again."

Summer took the parrot to the window and he flew away again.

"Is he yours?" asked Ella. "He's very beautiful."

"Yes, he's mine," said Summer. "He's supposed to stay in the bird house but he doesn't seem to like it down there. He's used to roaming free at home and now

16

there are all these rules."

The bedroom door swung open and an older girl marched in. Her pointed face was framed by thin dark hair. "Have you brought that bird inside again? I told you before: it's NOT allowed! Only cats and dogs are allowed up here."

"Do you mean Kanga the parrot, Molly?" said Lottie. "There are no birds in here. Look – no birds at all!"

The older girl looked around, frowning. "Well, make sure you don't bring him up here. The rules say no birds!" She muttered something about new girls, then – with an extra glare at Ella – she closed the door.

Lottie sighed. "That's Molly," she told Ella. "She's one of the Seahorse Tower captains. There are four of them – all older girls – in charge of this tower."

"The other captains seem lovely but

Molly just wants to boss everyone around all the time," said Summer.

"You see! That's why we can't ask just anyone to join," said Rosalind. "Molly would be awful as part of the—" She stopped suddenly and glanced at Ella.

Ella noticed the other girls exchanging looks. What had Rosalind been about to say? Ask everyone to join what?

Summer coughed awkwardly. "So what pet did you bring, Ella?"

"I..." Ella looked confused. "I didn't bring a pet. Is everyone allowed to keep one?"

"Oh yes! Every princess brings an animal with them. That's what the pet barn is for," said Lottie in surprise. "As long as it's not something too difficult to look after. I mean, they wouldn't be happy if you brought an elephant or something. It would be way too big!"

"Did you all bring animals with you?" Ella twisted the sleeve of her school jumper.

"I brought Kanga, my parrot," explained Summer.

"I brought a little hamster called Fluff," said Rosalind.

"And I brought my pony called Strawberry," added Lottie. "I couldn't bear to be away from her for long. I love riding her."

"Oh," said Ella.

"Didn't you have a pet that you wanted to bring?" asked Lottie.

Ella thought of her beautiful puppy, Sesame, who she'd left at home in his soft doggie bed. She swallowed. "No one said I was allowed to bring a pet. My mum told me lots about coming to school here because she came here too, a long time ago. But I guess they didn't have a pet

barn back then."

Just then there was a knock at the door and a girl with two brown plaits came in. "The postman's just arrived! Lottie and Summer, there are letters for you downstairs. Rosalind, I think you've got a parcel."

"Great!" Rosalind rushed to the door. "Do you want to stay here and settle in, Ella? We won't be long."

"Sure!" said Ella. "I'll wait here."

As they disappeared down the corridor, Ella heard Summer saying, "I think we should be careful who we tell about You Know What!"

Then the girls turned a corner and Ella couldn't hear any more. She pushed a lock of dark hair behind her ear. It seemed like there was something the other princesses didn't want her to know. Sighing, she walked over to the

bedroom window.

Below her were the school playing fields. A tall fence marked the edge of the school grounds and then the grass sloped down to a steep cliff. Beyond the cliff, the sea shimmered as sunlight danced on the waves. A handful of rocks jutted out of the water, guarded by a tall orange-and-white-striped lighthouse. For a moment Ella thought she could hear a faint song drifting on the wind.

She stared at the sea for a while. Somewhere beyond those waves was her home but it was thousands of miles away. And now she'd found out she was going to be the only one in the whole school without a pet to play with.

"Ella? Are you all right?"

Ella swung round and saw that Rosalind had come back in without her noticing. She took a deep breath and

tried to smile.

"I came to get you! You need to come downstairs straight away." Rosalind grabbed her hand. "Lottie and Summer and I have a surprise for you. I think you're going to like it!"

Chapter Three

The Pet Barn

Ella raced along the corridor after Rosalind. They ran downstairs to the balcony with the bronze bell. Rosalind began pointing things out as they passed. "The music and the art room are down that corridor," she said breathlessly. "And the staff room's there too."

They carried on down the next set of stairs to the entrance hall.

"I promise I'll show you round properly later on," added Rosalind. "There's the hall – you've seen that, haven't you?"

Ella nodded. "Where do we go for lessons?"

"There are lots of classrooms and a science lab around here somewhere," said Rosalind, waving her arm. "I get a bit lost sometimes because there are so many rooms. That door with the purple crown painted on it is the Throne Room where we do our Royal Skills classes."

Ella glanced curiously at the door with the purple crown. Her mum had told her a lot about the Royal Skills classes. Those were the lessons where you practised behaving in a royal manner – learning to bow and curtsy.

"Come on! We can look at all that later." Rosalind pulled her out of the front door and they ran across the garden together.

"Where are we going?" said Ella.

Rosalind grinned. "You'll see!"

They ran past a row of greenhouses. Then Ella saw Lottie and Summer waving at them from the doorway of a long, wooden barn.

"This is so exciting!" called Lottie. "I wish I was getting one too!"

Ella's brow wrinkled. "What do you mean? Getting what?"

Summer giggled and stood back from the doorway. "Come inside and we'll show you."

Ella stepped into the shadowy barn. At first she couldn't see much. What was that smell? It made her think of hay and animals.

Rosalind switched on a light. "Welcome to the pet barn!"

"Oh!" Ella stared round the barn in delight. There were pens on one side and rows of smaller hutches on the other.

A lamb bleated right next to her, making her jump. The little animal stuck its head over the side of its pen and looked at her nosily.

"What do you think?" said Rosalind, beaming.

"Wow! This is great!" said Ella. "I've never seen so many animals in one place."

"There are guinea pigs, gerbils and hamsters here, as well as the sheep and chickens which belong to the school," explained Lottie. "Cats and dogs are allowed upstairs in the bedrooms as long as they're well behaved, and ponies like my Strawberry live in the stables."

"Birds live in the bird house next door and that's where my parrot Kanga is meant to be," said Summer. "Except that he keeps on escaping to come and find me!"

"Hello, girls!" A lady with freckled

cheeks wearing jeans and wellies came into the barn. "Ah, is this someone new?" She smiled at Ella.

"I'm Ella," said Ella shyly. "I arrived today."

"Lovely to meet you!" the lady replied, brushing mud off her hands. "I'm Rebecca. I look after the pet barn and make sure that all the animals are happy and well looked after. Did you bring a pet with you?"

Ella shook her head sadly.

"But that's the good news!" Rosalind burst out. "We told Miss Goldwin that you hadn't got a pet and she said you could choose one of the new baby rabbits and look after it!"

"Really?" said Ella.

"Yes, really!" said Rosalind, grinning.

Ella's heart lifted. "Oh, thanks! That's amazing!"

"It was Rosalind's idea," said Lottie. "Then Summer found Miss Goldwin and I asked her if it was OK."

"That sounds like excellent teamwork," said Rebecca, smiling. "I hope you enjoy choosing a bunny, Ella. I must get on now – the horses need feeding." With a quick wave, she headed out of the barn.

"Bye, Rebecca!" called the princesses.

"Can I choose a rabbit right now?" asked Ella.

"Of course you can! I'll show you where they are." Rosalind skipped down the barn, avoiding a bucket of water that stood by the sheep pen.

Summer and Lottie ran after her and they stopped next to a large hutch that was full of hay.

"Come and look, Ella," said Summer. "You're going to love these bunnies. They're so cute!"

Chapter Four

Daisy the
Baby Rabbit

Ella hurried to join the others and
crouched down in front of the hutch.
There was no movement inside. A bundle
of small fluffy shapes lay huddled
together in a dark corner. "They're
sleeping!" she whispered.

"They were born a few weeks ago just
before the start of term," Rosalind told
her. "There are five of them altogether."

Summer undid the catch on the door.
"There you are! You can stroke them if

30

you like."

"Aw! They're lovely." Ella reached in and gently touched the rabbits. Their fur was warm and soft. There were two brown ones, two grey ones and a honey-coloured one with a little pink nose.

"Which one would you like?" said Lottie. "None of them even have names yet."

The rabbits opened their eyes at the sound of the girls' voices. The grey ones pricked up their ears. The honey-coloured rabbit hopped along the run. Then she looked up at Ella and twitched her pink nose.

"I'd like this one." Ella pointed to her. "And I'd like to call her..." She thought for a moment. "I'd like to call her Daisy."

"That's a pretty name!" Rosalind carefully lifted the honey-coloured rabbit out of the hutch and gave her to Ella.

"Hello, Daisy. You're so cute!" Ella stroked the bunny's floppy ears and they felt like velvet. Daisy's nose twitched and she wriggled a little. Ella smiled and pressed her cheek against the bunny's soft fur.

"She likes you!" said Lottie, grinning.

"I like her too," said Ella. "I'm glad I'm not going to be the only one here without a pet."

Just then there were heavy footsteps outside the barn and a girl with thin, dark hair came in. Ella recognised her. It was Molly, the girl who'd complained about Summer's parrot.

"Didn't you hear the bell for dinner?" snapped the older girl. "It went ten minutes ago. Miss Goldwin made me come and find you."

"No, we didn't hear it," said Lottie. "Thanks for telling us, Molly."

32

Molly ignored Lottie's thanks. She folded her arms and glared at them. "Who said you could take one of the rabbits out of their hutch? No one's allowed to touch them yet."

"Miss Goldwin said we could," said Rosalind. "This one belongs to Ella now."

Molly snorted. "Poor rabbit! I bet you don't know anything about looking after it. You're not even holding it right."

"Oh! Well, I've never had a rabbit before but I will look after her really carefully." Ella bit her lip. She didn't want the older girl to be cross with her. She just wanted to make friends. "Would you like to hold her? You can show me how to do it."

She walked towards Molly, but as she got closer Daisy wriggled frantically. Ella clutched at the little rabbit, afraid she was going to leap out of her arms.

Her foot caught on a bale of hay and she tripped, bumping into the older girl.

"Watch it!" Molly stepped backwards, knocking over the bucket of water by the sheep pen.

Water gushed everywhere. The metal bucket rolled across the ground with a hollow clang. Molly slipped, her arms flapping. Then she landed on her bottom on the wet floor.

"Are you OK?" Ella wanted to help the older girl but Daisy was still wriggling.

"Here you go! Take my hand." Lottie held out her arm but Molly wouldn't take it.

The older girl leapt to her feet, her face bright red. Her skirt and jumper were soaking, and bits of hay and dirt were stuck to her clothes. "Ugh! I'm wet and muddy, and it's all your fault!"

"I'm really sorry!" Ella felt her cheeks

flush. "I didn't mean to bump into you."

"You *will* be sorry!" hissed Molly. "I'm going to make you all wish you'd never come to this Academy. I'm a captain and I can stop you coming down to the pet barn if I want to!" She gave them a final glare and walked off.

Rosalind's eyes were fierce. "I don't know why she has to be like that! I'm going to tell Miss Goldwin what she said."

"Don't!" said Lottie. "It'll just make things worse."

"Are you all right, Ella?" said Summer. "Don't worry, it was just an accident."

"I know," said Ella. "I just wish I hadn't been so clumsy." She gave Daisy one more stroke and put her back with the other little bunnies. "I'll come back and see you really soon," she told the baby rabbit.

She hoped the older girl, Molly, didn't

really plan to stop them coming to the pet barn. She wanted to spend time with her new baby rabbit more than anything!

Chapter Five

Sharing a Secret

Over the next few days, Ella settled in to life at Harebell Castle. She got used to sharing a bunk bed with Summer in their room in Seahorse Tower and she even liked the school dinners, which always finished with a large helping of pudding!

With the help of Rebecca, who looked after the pet barn, she had learned all about taking care of baby rabbits. She knew what food Daisy needed and how often to clean her out. The princesses

were meant to check on their pets every morning and night. It wasn't easy as school life was very busy and Molly, the dark-haired captain, seemed to think of lots of jobs for Ella and her friends to do.

Ella liked her new teachers too. The only one who made her nervous was Lady Eggley, the Royal Skills teacher, who had perfectly smooth hair and eyes as sharp as needles. At first, Ella had liked going into the magnificent Throne Room for her lessons. The shelves were full of silver trophies, and the golden throne gleamed as if it was polished every day. But Lady Eggley swooped down on Ella every time she made a little mistake, telling Ella that her curtsies were terrible and her tiara always wonky.

Ella began to dread the Royal Skills lessons and talked to the others about it back in Seahorse Tower.

"Don't worry about it," said Lottie. "Lady Eggley is a right royal fusspot."

"I've heard that she's madly keen on eating carrots and always keeps some in her bedroom," said Rosalind. "Maybe her name should be Lady Carroty instead of Lady Eggley."

Ella giggled, feeling a little better.

Summer put down her reading book and climbed off the top bunk. "Now we're all together, why don't we go down to the pet barn and see the animals? You can check on your rabbit, Ella, and we can look at the other baby bunnies too."

The door swung open and Molly stood there, smiling meanly. "Oh good! You're all here. I need you to help with some chores."

"But we were just going down to check on our pets," protested Ella. "We don't want Rebecca to think we're not looking

after them properly."

"No, Rebecca wouldn't be pleased if you didn't take care of your rabbit," said Molly, with a spiteful look in her eye. "But first, all the rooms in the tower need dusting and the corridor needs sweeping. Hurry up now!" And she slammed the door.

"Every time we try to go to the pet barn, she invents a job for us," said Lottie. "I haven't seen Strawberry for three days. If this carries on, Rebecca will have to report us to Miss Goldwin for not looking after our animals. We might not even be allowed to keep our pets any more. We *have* to get away from Molly!"

"I wish her room wasn't right at the start of the corridor," said Summer. "No one can leave the tower without her seeing."

Rosalind folded her arms. "We can beat

her easily. All we need are some ninja moves."

"Some what?" said Ella, surprised.

Rosalind put her hand over her mouth. "Oops!"

Lottie rolled her eyes. "You've said it now, Rosalind! I think we should tell you our secret anyway, Ella. You're one of us now."

Ella turned pink. "Thanks, Lottie!"

"Let's explain later. We don't want Molly hearing," said Summer.

So, after dinner, they found an empty classroom downstairs instead of returning to Seahorse Tower. Rosalind took out her torch. "Don't switch the lights on. We don't want anyone to know we're in here."

Ella felt a swooping in her stomach. Now she would find out what the secret was!

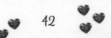

"First of all you have to promise not to tell anyone about this," said Lottie.

Ella nodded quickly. "I won't tell."

Rosalind took a deep breath. "You see, we're the Rescue Princesses and we rescue animals in danger."

"I was the first one to set up the club," said Lottie. "Well, it was my sister, Emily, actually. She rescued some deer in Mistberg Forest with the help of her friends. But when she left to go to school, I took over."

"That's when I joined," added Rosalind. "It was me, Lottie, Amina and Isabella. You haven't met Amina and Isabella because they're not coming here till next term."

"Then I met everyone in the springtime," said Summer. "We rescued a snow leopard with the help of a princess called Maya."

"So you'll be the twelfth Rescue Princess," said Lottie. "But the number isn't really important. The point is we help animals, no matter how dangerous it is, and we have magic jewels that help us *and* we know ninja moves too! We even have a book about ninja moves hidden upstairs."

"Wow!" Ella stared at them all. "That is so cool."

"So would you like to join?" said Lottie.

"Yes, please!" Ella beamed. "It sounds very exciting."

"Good! So tomorrow we'll use our ninja moves to get past Molly," said Lottie, pushing back her red curls. "We'll wait till lessons are finished and then sneak out before she can stop us."

"Oh, one more thing!" said Rosalind. "I made a few more rings in the holidays just in case we needed them and yours is a yellow diamond." She dropped a ring with a beautiful yellow jewel into Ella's hand. "Pressing the jewel lets us talk to each other."

"Thank you!" Ella slid the ring on to her finger and pressed the diamond. The jewel lit up instantly and the rings on her friends' hands shone brightly too. Lottie had a ruby ring, Rosalind had a deep-blue sapphire and Summer's jewel was a beautiful purple amethyst.

The princesses were still admiring their magical rings when the door creaked open. Ella swung round and was dazzled when someone switched on the light.

"Hey! What's going on?" said a voice.

The girls leapt up. Lottie and Summer stuffed their hands behind their backs to hide their glowing rings. Ella tripped over a chair and grabbed hold of a table to stop herself falling over.

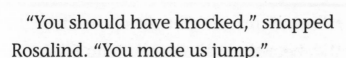

"You should have knocked," snapped
Rosalind. "You made us jump."

Ella got her balance back and turned
round, worried that Molly had found
them.

There were five girls standing in the
doorway and thankfully none of them
was Molly. The girl at the front had long
red curls and looked familiar somehow.

"Emily!" said Lottie.

The girl with the red curls grinned. "Hi,
little sis! Sorry we made you jump. We
heard voices and wondered what was
going on. What were you doing in the
dark?"

"We're inviting a new girl into the
Rescue Princesses," said Lottie. "It's
OK!" she told the others. "These are the
old members of the gang. This is Lulu,
Clarabel, Jaminta, Freya and my sister
Emily. They all belong to Coral Tower."

The older princesses smiled. "We heard you'd carried on the Rescue Princesses and had lots of adventures," said a girl with black hair and lion-like eyes. "Well done!"

"Thanks, Lulu," said Lottie. "Actually, we're organising a mission right now." And she told the older girls about the problem with Molly and what had happened in the pet barn.

"Molly's being so unfair," added Rosalind. "So we're going to use our ninja moves to get out of Seahorse Tower and away from her! Otherwise we can't look after our pets properly."

Emily looked a bit worried. "Well, be careful when you're sneaking around! I've heard that this castle has hidden doors and secret passages!"

"That's right," nodded Lulu. "After all, this place was a proper castle in the olden

days before it became a school!"

"I wish we could find some of the secret places," said Lottie. "Then we could hide from Molly and her endless list of chores!"

"Do take care, little sis," Emily said to Lottie. "You have such a way of getting into trouble."

"Oh, don't worry!" said Lottie. "We're not babies. We know exactly what to do!"

Chapter Six

The Ninja
Bumblebee

The next day crept by slowly. At last,
lessons ended and the four girls hurried
back to Seahorse Tower.

Once the bedroom door was closed,
Rosalind lifted up her mattress and took
out a book hidden underneath. It had a
black cover with *Book of Ninja* written on
it in gold letters. Ella noticed how old it
looked. Some of the pages were worn and
speckled with brown marks.

"I had a quick look last night and

I think I've found the perfect thing," said Rosalind, flicking through the pages. "This move will give us a way of distracting Molly while we sneak out." She turned the book round to show them.

The picture showed someone dangling a shoe out of a window using a piece of string. Another picture showed the person in the room below looking out of the window at the floating shoe in amazement.

"So we can surprise Molly and make her stare out of the window while we escape," said Summer. "There's a bathroom above her bedroom so we should be able to get in there easily."

"But what shall we put on the end of the string?" said Lottie. "If we're not careful she'll realise that it's a trick straight away."

"We could dangle one of our teddies,"

suggested Summer.

"I'm not dangling mine." Lottie tucked her teddy under her arm. "He might fall off!"

"It should be something that's supposed to fly," said Ella. "Then she'll think it's real. Something like a butterfly or a— I know!" She jumped to her feet, opened a drawer and pulled out a pair of stripy black-and-yellow socks. "A bumblebee!"

"Ella! That's a great idea!" said Rosalind. "Those stripes do look like a bee. We can stuff the sock with paper and put wings on it. Then when Molly looks out of the window she'll wonder if she's seeing a giant bee."

There were heavy footsteps and the door opened. Ella quickly hid the stripy socks behind her back.

Molly looked in and scowled. "There'll be a room inspection in ten minutes so

don't think you can run off anywhere."

"Molly, I just want to visit my rabbit today," began Ella. "Do you think—"

"Forget it!" snapped Molly. "You haven't got time!" And she closed the door with a bang.

Lottie waited a moment and then opened the door a crack and checked that the older girl had gone. "That's it, then! She's had her chance. Let's put together our ninja trick."

Together, they stuffed one of the socks with paper to give the bee a round body. Then Summer found two pieces of clear plastic that they cut into wing shapes and stuck on with sticky tape.

Ella fetched her sewing kit and took out a blue cotton reel. "If we use blue-coloured thread then hopefully she won't spot it. The cotton will be camouflaged against the sky."

"Be as quick as you can," urged Rosalind. "Molly will be back any minute."

Finally, the fake bumblebee was ready.

"I'll take the bee up to the bathroom and dangle it from the window," said Rosalind. "You three go ahead and sneak out. I'll catch up with you in the pet barn." Stuffing the bee under her jumper, Rosalind ran swiftly upstairs.

"OK, is everyone ready?" whispered Lottie. "Let's get a bit closer."

Ella, Lottie and Summer tiptoed down the corridor. They heard heavy footsteps inside Molly's room. Lottie signalled for them to stop but the older girl didn't come out into the corridor. They crept even closer and peeped round the door.

Molly was standing in front of the mirror doing different poses. She put her hands on her hips. Then she folded her

arms and grinned at the mirror. Ella had the urge to giggle and clapped her hand over her mouth.

There was a soft tapping sound. A yellow-and-black stripy bee-sock swung through the air and thudded gently against the window.

Ella had a sudden brainwave. "I know what will help," she murmured to Summer.

Whump! The bee-sock bumped against the window again. Molly caught sight of it and swung round.

"Bzzzzz!" Ella began making a soft buzzing sound. "Bzz, bzz!"

Molly stepped closer to the window. "Huh! What's going on?"

"Bzz!" Ella got a bit louder, and Summer and Lottie joined in.

The bee-sock outside the window began bobbing up and down in the air, as if it

was doing a little bumblebee dance.

Molly ran to the window, opened it and stuck her head out. The bee-sock soared over her head into the sky. "No way! That bee was enormous!"

With one final buzz, Ella, Lottie and Summer raced past the doorway and down the corridor. They ran until they reached the bottom of the stairs, then they collapsed into giggles.

"She thought it was real!" gasped Summer.

"I bet she'll tell everyone she saw the biggest bee in the world!" snorted Lottie.

"It was a shame the bee had to buzz off in the end!" giggled Ella.

Still laughing, they made their way out of school and across the garden to the pet barn. Lottie ran off to the stables to see her pony, Strawberry, while Ella and Summer went to visit the rabbits. The barn was dark and cosy. Animals rustled in the hay and now and then the lambs bleated.

"Rebecca's not here," said Summer, looking around. "Maybe she's busy in the fields."

"I hope Daisy still remembers me," said Ella.

"Of course she will," replied Summer. "It's only been a few days. She wouldn't forget you that quickly."

They crouched down next to the rabbit run. The two grey rabbits were asleep in a corner and the brown ones were nibbling on some hay. Daisy was standing by the side of the pen, her little pink nose tilted upwards as if she'd been waiting for them.

"Hello, Daisy." Ella leaned over and stroked her honey-coloured fur.

Daisy twitched her nose at Ella's hand

and hopped up and down the run in excitement. Ella laughed. Then as soon as the little bunny stopped jumping, she lifted her out of the run for a cuddle.

"Aw, she's lovely!" Summer rubbed Daisy's ears. "I'm just going to see the hens. I want to know if any chicks have hatched today."

Ella smiled. "Call me if you see any." She sat down on a hay bale and rested Daisy in her lap. "Next time I come I'm going to bring you a treat," she told the little rabbit. "Would you like some carrots? I wish you could live in my bedroom with me. That would be so awesome."

Suddenly Daisy pricked up her ears. Then she stood up on her hind legs, sniffing the air.

"What is it?" said Ella. "Can you smell something strange?"

Daisy huddled up and hid her nose under Ella's arm.

Puzzled, Ella got up, holding tight to her rabbit. She crossed to the barn window and looked out.

Molly was striding across the lawn with a huge frown on her face.

"Oh no!" whispered Ella. "She must have worked out that we sneaked away. We have to hide!"

Chapter Seven

The Wonders of the Throne Room

Ella hurried down the barn, calling to Summer as loudly as she dared. Summer poked her head out of the henhouse.

"Molly's coming," hissed Ella. "We've got to do something!"

"I'll go this way." Summer pointed to the back door. "I'll find Lottie and we'll meet you back at Seahorse Tower."

Ella nodded. Through the window, she could see Molly getting closer. She dashed out of the main door and ran

61

along the side of the barn until she came to a wooden bench. She crouched down behind it, hoping that Molly hadn't spotted her running from the barn.

Daisy wriggled in her arms. Ella stroked the rabbit's soft ears. In her panic about Molly, she'd almost forgotten that she was holding the little bunny.

Molly marched straight inside without looking in the direction of the bench. Ella got up from her hiding place and tiptoed back to the barn door. Molly was leaning over the rabbit pen, counting the number of baby rabbits. Then she sat down on a hay bale and folded her arms.

She's waiting till I come back, thought Ella.

Nervously, she pushed a black curl behind her ear and wondered what to do. She had to talk to the others. They would have some ideas for a ninja move. With

one last look at the barn, she rushed across the garden, darting behind the privet statues and hoping she wouldn't be seen.

Luckily, the castle entrance was empty. Ella hurried towards the stairs, stopping when she heard Lady Eggley's voice drifting down from the balcony. "There's such a terrible draught in this castle! Why must the princesses always leave the front door wide open? I shall close it myself!"

Ella's eyes widened. If a teacher caught her bringing a rabbit into the castle, she'd be in big trouble. And Lady Eggley was the very last teacher she wanted to be caught by! Looking left and right, Ella darted through the nearest open door into the Throne Room.

She heard Lady Eggley's high-heeled shoes tapping on the stone floor outside.

Where could she hide? The room was quite bare, with just a strip of red carpet leading to the magnificent golden throne. Pictures of kings and queens hung on the walls and the shelves had rows of silver trophies.

Ella spotted a small door in the corner of the room. She thought it must be a store cupboard. She ran to it and pulled the handle. It was locked. Quickly, she ducked down behind the golden throne before she was seen. Her heart thumped and she hugged Daisy tightly.

"Lady Eggley, I have some bad news." Molly's voice rang out clearly.

Ella peeked round the throne and looked through the open doorway. She saw Molly standing next to the teacher in the hallway outside. She watched the older girl curtsy perfectly. Ella stifled a sigh. Why couldn't she curtsy like that?

"What is it, Molly?" said Lady Eggley. "Nothing serious I hope."

"I've just seen a new girl bring a rabbit into the castle," said Molly in a shocked voice. "Her name is Ella. I'm afraid that as a captain in her tower I find her very badly behaved."

Lady Eggley's eyebrows rose and she tutted.

"And her fingernails are really dirty," added Molly.

Ella looked at her fingernails. She had to admit they were quite grubby.

"Well, there is no excuse for that!" declared Lady Eggley. "Find her and bring her straight to me. I shall wait here."

Ella peered round the edge of the golden throne again. She could still see Lady Eggley standing in the hallway outside. The teacher frowned and smoothed her perfect hair.

Ella shifted uncomfortably. Her legs were aching and Daisy was wriggling, but she knew if she stood up she'd be seen. She hoped that Lady Eggley would get tired of waiting in one place and walk off, giving her the chance to escape.

Summer and Lottie came running through the front door into the hallway.

"Princesses! You must *not* run inside the Academy," said Lady Eggley.

"Sorry!" Summer dropped a curtsy.

"Have either of you seen a princess named Ella and a runaway rabbit?" demanded Lady Eggley.

"No, sorry!" said Lottie. "We don't know where she is."

"Well, if you see her please send her to me. I shall not permit animals and princesses to run wild!" said the teacher. Then she muttered to herself, "This is what comes of turning Harebell Castle into a pet club."

Ella heard Lottie and Summer walk away but Lady Eggley remained in the hallway, tapping one high-heeled shoe. Ella looked down at Daisy and saw that she'd fallen asleep.

To try and take her mind off her aching legs, Ella gazed at the ornate carvings on the golden throne. Being so close, she could see every shape and swirl. Little red rubies sparkled along the throne's arms and green emeralds glistened on the top. A red velvet cloth wrapped around the lower part of the throne and reached down to the floor.

Ella gazed at the small shells carved into the back of the throne. They were so beautiful! One shell gleamed more brightly than the others and she traced her finger across its fan-like shape.

Then, suddenly, the shell moved.

Ella paused; surely she must have imagined it! Slowly, she touched the golden shell again and pushed it.

The shell moved smoothly to the side. There was a muffled clunk from the corner, and the door of the cupboard swung slightly open.

Ella turned and stared. Golden light poured through the crack in the door. It couldn't be a cupboard... But then, what was it? And how had this golden shell unlocked it?

A tingle ran down her back.

"What's that noise?" said Lady Eggley.

Ella peered over the top of the throne. The teacher was looking all around the hall. She must have heard the clunking noise as the door opened! What if she came into the Throne Room? Ella's heart thumped and she pushed the shell again.

She had to close the door quickly. But the door wouldn't move.

Ella tried again. She put Daisy down on the floor so that she could use both hands. The little rabbit woke up and twitched her nose. Ella pushed the shell with all her strength.

This time it moved a little. The door swung back until it was almost shut and only a tiny glint of light could be seen. Ella was just about to reach across and close the door completely when Lady Eggley marched into the room.

"Who's there?" said the teacher. "I demand that you come out at once."

Ella's heart sank. Quickly, she hid Daisy underneath the red cloth that circled the bottom of the throne. Then she took a deep breath and stood up. "Hello, Lady Eggley." She gave a wobbly curtsy. "It's me, Princess Ella."

Chapter Eight

Ella in Trouble

Lady Eggley looked Ella up and down, a deep frown creasing her forehead.

Ella suddenly realised how dusty her skirt looked and that bits of hay were sticking to her jumper. "Um, I can explain—" she began.

"You can *explain*!" screeched Lady Eggley. "Nothing you say can excuse such unruly behaviour! This is *not* what we expect of our princesses."

Ella's cheeks flushed. "I'm really sorry."

"Hiding like that – such cheek! And just look at the state of you!" Lady Eggley took hold of Ella's hand and examined her fingernails.

Just then, Molly ran into the room. "Oh, Lady Eggley. You've found her." She cast a mean grin at Ella behind the teacher's back. "But where's the rabbit?"

Ella hoped that Daisy was still hidden under the red cloth behind the throne.

Lady Eggley's attention was still fixed on Ella's fingernails. "You must learn to scrub these nails thoroughly. Do it at least twenty times a day!" She let go of Ella's hand. "Now, unless you have some good reason for being in here, I shall have to find you a punishment."

Molly's grin widened.

"Did someone say punishment?" Rebecca walked in. Her eyes flicked from Ella's worried face to Molly's grin.

"I'm afraid that Ella has been very naughty." Lady Eggley brushed a speck of dust from her sleeve. "She came in here by herself without permission. She hid from me and she is *not* clean and tidy. Therefore I shall be deciding on a suitable punishment for her."

"Excellent!" said Rebecca firmly. "I need someone to help me carry lots of bags of hay. That can be Ella's punishment. I'm sure you won't object, Lady Eggley; I really need the extra help."

"Of course!" said the teacher graciously. "I will leave her in your charge. And remember, Princess Ella, I shall be checking your fingernails from now on." She nodded to Rebecca and swept from the room.

Molly glanced round the room again and Ella knew she was still looking for Daisy.

"Run along then, Molly," said Rebecca.

Molly looked annoyed but had no choice but to go.

Rebecca turned to Ella and smiled. "Are you all right, Ella? I saw your friends outside the pet barn just now and they told me all about how difficult Molly has been. I'd started to think you didn't want to look after your little rabbit but I hear that isn't true."

"It isn't true at all!" cried Ella. "I really *do* want to take care of Daisy. It was awful when Molly wouldn't give us time to come down to the barn." Her eyes flicked sideways, expecting to catch a glimpse of the rabbit. Where *was* Daisy?

"Well, Lady Eggley is expecting you to help me so we'd better head to the barn," said Rebecca. "Moving the hay is actually quite a nice job, I think! And you'll be able to say hello to your bunny again."

Ella flushed. She knew she should explain to Rebecca that her rabbit was here in the Throne Room but what if the pet keeper was really shocked? What if she was so cross that she wouldn't let her keep Daisy any more?

Ella decided she should be honest. "Um, the thing is," she began. "I left the pet barn in a bit of a hurry and—"

"Oh, don't worry!" said Rebecca. "If you'd rather help carry the hay tomorrow then that's fine. It doesn't have to be done today. I won't tell Lady Eggley if you don't!" She gave Ella a wink.

Ella swallowed. Rebecca hadn't really understood.

Just then, Lottie, Summer and Rosalind ran in. "There you are!" said Rosalind. "We were beginning to think you'd vanished."

"Hello, girls! Well, I must get on."

Rebecca marched to the door. "There are ponies to feed and groom, hamsters to clean out and goodness knows what else!" And she was gone before Ella could say anything more.

"What happened, Ella?" said Lottie. "We couldn't see you anywhere."

"I was here all the time but I had to hide when Lady Eggley stood outside in the hallway." Ella dived behind the throne to look for her rabbit.

"Are you OK?" said Rosalind, watching her in surprise.

"I have to find Daisy. She's somewhere round here." Ella pulled up the red material that circled the bottom of the throne and felt around underneath. Her fingers swept across empty floorboards. She crouched right down behind the throne and put her head under the red cloth.

There was nothing there.

"Daisy! Where are you?" Ella looked around frantically. "I put her here. She can't have just disappeared!"

The other girls peered underneath the red cloth too.

"She can't be very far. There's nowhere else to hide," said Summer.

The girls spread out, checking behind chairs and even on the trophy shelves.

Ella suddenly remembered the golden shell and the mysterious door. "Oh, I nearly forgot!" She ran to the corner. "I thought this was a locked cupboard but when I pushed one shell on the back of the throne the door opened like magic. I tried to close it but..." She caught her breath. The door was only open a tiny crack but it was still large enough for a baby rabbit to squeeze through.

"You mean the door opens with a magic

switch?" said Lottie. "I'd like to see that!"

Ella pulled the door open and golden light poured through. Inside was an alcove with an old-fashioned lantern. The light from the lantern shone on to a stone passage that curved away around a corner.

"Wow!" Rosalind gasped, peering into the passageway.

"I wonder where it leads," said Summer.

"Poor Daisy!" said Ella. "She must have squeezed through when no one was looking. We have to find her."

Bong! The castle bell rang out three times and then footsteps came down the hallway. Ella closed the mysterious door quickly and stood in front of it.

Molly came in. "That was the bell for dinner," she told them. "Hurry up – or I'll tell Lady Eggley that you were messing around in here again."

Rosalind squeezed Ella's hand and whispered. "Don't worry! We'll come back."

Ella followed the others out of the room. She knew Molly was watching her and she tried hard not to look back at the door. *I'll explore that secret passage once Molly's not looking!* she told herself fiercely. *She won't stop me finding Daisy.*

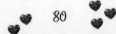

Chapter Nine

The Hidden Passageway

Dinner was a delicious cheese and tomato pizza with salad but Ella didn't taste any of it. She gulped down her food, while the others whispered about fetching torches from upstairs.

"That lantern inside the door might not light the whole passageway," said Rosalind. "We need to take torches just in case."

Ella could see Molly sitting at a table nearby and caught the older girl looking at her a few times.

When they'd finished, Summer went back for the torches. The other girls hung around the entrance hall, waiting for a chance to slip into the Throne Room without anyone seeing.

Ella linked her fingers together, trying to stop her hands from shaking. She couldn't bear the thought of Daisy all alone in the stone passageway. She hoped they would find her quickly.

Summer returned with the torches but it took a long time for all the other girls to leave the dining hall and go upstairs to their towers. At last the hallway emptied. The princesses slipped into the Throne Room without switching on the light, and closed the door behind them.

Ella went behind the throne and fumbled for the golden shell. "Here it is!" She pushed the shell and it slid sideways.

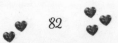

The Golden Shell

There was a muffled clunk and the door in the corner swung open. Light poured into the room from the old-fashioned lantern on the alcove inside.

"Quickly!" hissed Rosalind. "Let's go before someone comes in and finds us!"

The girls bundled into the stone passage and Lottie closed the door behind them.

"Wait, Lottie!" said Summer. "What if there isn't a way to open the door from this side?"

"There must be!" said Lottie.

The girls looked at the door but there was no handle on the inside and no lever on the wall either.

"Er...sorry!" said Lottie. "I didn't mean to shut us in. But there'll be a way out at the other end, right?"

The others looked at each other worriedly.

Then Ella said, "There must be another

way out. Let's just find Daisy."

Rosalind led the way along the stone corridor. After the first bend, the light from the lantern faded and the girls switched on their torches. Ella shone hers at the floor, hoping to see Daisy leaping along passage in front of them. She longed to find the little bunny and stroke her warm fur.

The passageway twisted again and again. The princesses followed it left and right, and their feet began to ache.

"I didn't think we'd have to walk so far," said Lottie. "It seems like we've been in here for a long time."

"Ooh, look at the ceiling," said Summer, shining her torch upwards. "There are golden shells up there that look just like the one on the back of the throne."

The other girls looked up. "You're right," said Ella. "They have the same fan

shape as the one that opened the mystery door. I hope that means we're going the right way."

They came to some steps and followed them downwards. At the bottom Rosalind stopped suddenly, making the others bump into her.

"Rosy! Don't stop like that!" cried Lottie.

"Shh!" said Rosalind. "I can hear something."

A low clanking noise came from above them, mixed with the sound of muffled voices.

"It sounds a bit like people washing up," said Ella at last. "Do you think we're below the kitchen?"

"Yes, we must be!" said Rosalind, her blue eyes gleaming. "And maybe that's why Daisy came down here. Maybe she smelled vegetables and she felt hungry!"

"Let's keep going," said Lottie.

They hurried along the narrow corridor. The stone floor became uneven and Ella noticed that the walls were damp. The passageway opened out into a small, empty room.

"Look!" Ella shone her torch at the door. "There's a way out and it has that golden shell on it again."

"Hold on!" Rosalind frowned. "Where's Daisy? She can't have turned the handle and opened that door."

"Look, there's a hole." Lottie shone her torch at a small gap at the bottom of the wall where a brick was missing. "I bet Daisy got out that way. It's just the right size for a rabbit!"

Ella crouched down close to the hole and caught the smell of cooking. "You're right – she could easily have gone through there."

Lottie pulled at the door but it didn't open. "It's stuck! Now what are we going to do?"

Rosalind tried the door too. "I hope it's not locked."

"Let's try pulling it at the same time," suggested Ella, and she and Rosalind both took hold of the door handle.

"One, two, three, go!" said Rosalind, and they pulled together.

The door flew open, sending both girls flying backwards.

"Are you all right?" Summer asked, helping them up.

"I'm fine." Ella rubbed her elbow. "I just hope no one heard the noise."

"It's all right – there's no one here," said Lottie, who had gone through to look around. "It looks like this is some kind of store room."

The other princesses followed her into

the room, closing the door carefully behind them. The room was quite small and had no windows. Tall cupboards lined the walls and baskets of fruit and vegetables were stacked to one side. Stone steps led up to a half-open door, and beyond that was the sound of people talking and banging saucepans.

"We must be right next to the kitchens," muttered Rosalind.

"There's no sign of Daisy though." Summer shone her torch into the corners of the room.

"Poor Daisy!" said Ella. "I *wish* Molly hadn't stopped us from looking earlier. We might have found her straightaway." She ran up the steps to the half-open door, stopping when she heard a familiar voice.

"Where is my plate? I don't want to wait for ever, you know," said Lady Eggley snootily. "I've had a very busy day and I want to go to bed soon. Please hurry up and put my snacks on the trolley."

Ella's heart sank. Where was Daisy? If Lady Eggley caught sight of her they would all be in big trouble!

Chapter Ten

The Bunny Hunt

Ella signalled to the others to be quiet.
Then she peeped round the door. She
could see Lady Eggley and one of the
cooks, who was wearing a large green
apron. Next to Lady Eggley was a small
catering trolley with wheels. Ella tried to
see if there was anything on the trolley
but the teacher was blocking her view.

"Oh good. You've done it *at last*," said
Lady Eggley. "I shall wheel this to my
room now. Good night." Then she left the

kitchen, pushing the trolley in front of her. The click-clack of her footsteps grew fainter.

"Lady Eggley's gone," Ella whispered to the others.

"That lady has no manners," muttered the cook, banging a saucepan down on the table. "No manners at all! Now, what's all this? Who's made a mess of my lettuces?"

Rosalind nudged Ella. "Something's knocked over the box of lettuces – look!"

Ella saw the cook pick up the fallen lettuces and put them back in the box. "I bet that was Daisy!" she whispered. "Maybe she's hiding somewhere."

At last, the cook finished tidying up. She hung up her apron and switched off the light. As soon as she'd gone, the princesses switched their torches back on and dashed into the kitchen.

 93

They searched under tables and inside cupboards. They peered into the fridge and even took the lids off the saucepans to check inside.

"I can't think of anywhere else to look," said Rosalind.

"Where *are* you, Daisy?" Ella said softly.

"I don't think she's here," said Summer at last. "Maybe she knocked over those lettuces and then hopped away."

"She might have gone this way." Lottie hurried down the passageway and the others followed.

Ella felt an uneasy wriggling deep down in her tummy. She didn't know her way around the school very well and it was even more confusing in the dark. How had Daisy managed to hop so far without getting tired? She was only a baby rabbit after all!

"Here's the art room and next door is

the library," said Lottie. "Rosalind and Ella, you look in the library, and Summer and I will search in here."

Ella followed Rosalind into the library. The two girls went along every single shelf of books and checked carefully under the chairs and tables.

"This is really strange," said Ella, pushing back her dark, wavy hair.

"What do you mean?" said Rosalind.

"I don't understand how Daisy's come so far." Ella bit her lip. "It's as if she's just disappeared."

"It is a bit weird," agreed Rosalind. "But she must be somewhere."

Lottie opened the library door. "There are no bunnies in the art room. Any luck in here?"

Ella and Rosalind shook their heads.

The princesses carried on searching. They checked three classrooms and then tiptoed on into a new corridor with thick red carpets.

"Watch out, everyone," hissed Lottie. "This is where the teachers sleep."

"We should go back," said Summer. "We could get in so much trouble."

"Maybe we can take a peek inside their bedrooms?" Lottie tiptoed up to the nearest door and pulled down the handle. "I'll only open the door a tiny bit."

"Lottie!" gasped Ella. "What if the teacher wakes up and sees you looking in?"

There was a low snort from inside the room, followed by a voice saying. "Hmm? What's that? Your dirty fingernails are a disgrace!" Then there was a creaking sound followed by silence.

Lottie opened the door very slightly and there was another loud snort from

the bed. "I think that's Lady Eggley," she whispered with a giggle.

"Not so loud," muttered Rosalind.

Ella didn't dare to shine her torch into the room. She peered through the darkness. "It does look like Lady Eggley," she whispered to the others. "And look, there's the trolley that she wheeled out of the kitchens."

The trolley was covered by a long piece of cloth that gaped at one end, revealing another shelf underneath. Ella looked closer. Was that a small furry shape next to the trolley? "Daisy!" she whispered joyfully.

The furry shape twitched and two ears pricked up.

"Oh, Daisy! What are you doing in there?" murmured Summer.

"I bet she rode all the way here on the bottom of that trolley and Lady Eggley didn't even know," said Lottie, giggling. "She had no idea that she was giving a rabbit a ride!"

Rosalind nudged her. "Shh, Lottie! You're still too loud—" She broke off as the teacher turned over in bed.

Then a muffled voice said, "Wretched girls! I can hear them talking. They should NOT be running around in the middle of the night!"

Ella gasped and flapped her hand at Lottie. "Close the door!" she mouthed. "Quickly, before she sees us!"

Chapter Eleven

Lady Eggley's Bedroom

Lottie shut the teacher's door. The girls stood still, holding their breath and listening out for sounds from inside.

"I can't hear any creaking so I don't think she's got out of bed," whispered Summer. "Maybe she was just talking in her sleep."

"We need to get Daisy out of there," said Lottie. "If Lady Eggley catches the rabbit in her room she'll go crazy!"

"Can you get Daisy to come to you,

99

Ella?" said Summer. "She loves you. Maybe if she sees you she'll come over?"

"I'll try." Ella's heart thumped as she slowly pulled down the door handle.

Loud snores filled the bedroom and Ella felt relieved. Lady Eggley must be asleep. She saw Lottie put her fingers over her mouth to stop a giggle.

Kneeling down, Ella held out her hand and whispered as quietly as she could, "Daisy! Come over here." But the rabbit twitched her nose naughtily and bounced away behind the trolley.

Ella straightened up. "I'm going in to get her," she whispered to the others. "Rosalind, could you hold the door for me?"

Rosalind held the door open, wincing when it creaked a little. Ella crept over to the trolley but Daisy wasn't hiding there. She wasn't on the bottom shelf or behind

100

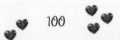

the dangling cloth.

Ella bit her lip. The longer it took to find the little rabbit, the more likely they all were to get caught. She tiptoed round the room, looking for Daisy on the floor. Then she knelt down and checked under the bed. She looked into all the corners and behind the wastepaper basket. She couldn't see Daisy anywhere.

Lady Eggley was still snoring. Now and then, she muttered something in her sleep.

Lottie came in and started looking too. Ella peered behind the perfume bottles and hand mirrors on the teacher's dressing table. She turned round, wondering where else to look. Something moved on the bed and Ella froze. On top of the sleeping teacher sat a little floppy-eared bunny!

"Can you see her?" hissed Lottie.

Ella put a finger to her lips and then pointed at Daisy, who was hopping along the blanket that covered Lady Eggley's legs.

"She must have jumped up there," whispered Lottie.

Ella wondered how she was going to pick up Daisy without waking the teacher. Lady Eggley grunted in her sleep and then smacked her lips together. Ella held her breath but the teacher didn't open her eyes.

Daisy hopped over Lady Eggley's stomach till she reached her neck. Then, to Ella's horror, she nibbled at the teacher's chin.

"What's that?" muttered Lady Eggley. "Tickling is not allowed in class!"

Ella ducked down and crawled across the floor to the bed. She had to get to Daisy before the bunny did something

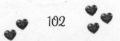

102

even naughtier! She peered at the
sleeping teacher just as the rabbit jumped
on to the pillow and began snuffling at
Lady Eggley's ear.

Ella tried to take hold of Daisy. Her
hand brushed against soft fur but the
bunny slipped under her fingers and
sprang off the pillow on to the bedside
table. Lady Eggley rolled over in bed.
Ella waited until the teacher had stopped
moving, then she crawled after Daisy.

A plate of carrot sticks lay on the
bedside table. Next to it was a yellow
book with the title *How to Look Elegant
and Impress a Gentleman.*

Lottie waved her arms and pointed
at the carrot sticks. "Lady Eggley loves
carrots," she whispered. "She must have
brought them here on the kitchen trolley.
I bet Daisy was after them too!"

Lady Eggley stirred at the sound of

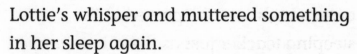

Lottie's whisper and muttered something in her sleep again.

Ella felt a fluttering in her tummy. If Lady Eggley woke up now she'd take them straight to the Headmistress!

Quickly, she reached over and took all the carrots off the plate. Daisy, who had nearly reached the vegetables, looked at her reproachfully. Crouching back down, Ella held the carrots close to the floor and edged backwards. After a moment, the little rabbit jumped down from the bedside table and followed the carrots.

Ella crawled backwards, holding the carrots out in front of her. She kept her eyes fixed on Daisy. Lottie tried to step out of Ella's way and bumped into the wardrobe, making it rattle.

Lady Eggley jerked in the bed. "The princesses forgot to curtsy? Someone must be punished!"

105

Ella's heart pounded so loud she wondered for a moment if everyone would hear it. Then the teacher dozed off again. Checking that Lottie was out of the way, Ella crept backwards with the carrots. Daisy hopped after her with her nose twitching. At last they reached the corridor and Ella gently picked up Daisy and hugged her tight. "Silly thing!" she murmured. "I was so worried about you."

Daisy twitched her nose. Then she took a carrot stick from Ella's hand and crunched it.

The princesses took Daisy upstairs to Seahorse Tower. They knew that the main doors of the castle were locked at night and they'd have to wait till morning to take the baby rabbit back to the pet barn. Ella didn't really mind. It gave her a chance for a longer cuddle with her bunny. She pressed her cheek against

Daisy's warm fur, glad that the baby animal was safe.

Summer found a small empty suitcase and padded it with a woolly scarf to make a comfortable sleeping place for Daisy.

"What a strange adventure!" yawned Summer. "It was amazing how that little golden shell opened up a whole secret passageway."

Lottie's eyes gleamed. "Maybe there are other golden shells hidden around the castle that will take us into more tunnels."

"Well, I'm definitely too tired to look for them tonight," said Rosalind. "My legs are aching. I feel like I've walked for miles and miles!"

"Me too," agreed Ella. "I'm really looking forward to getting into bed! I bet even Daisy's tired."

They all looked over at the baby rabbit snuggled up among the folds of the woolly scarf and saw that she'd fallen fast asleep.

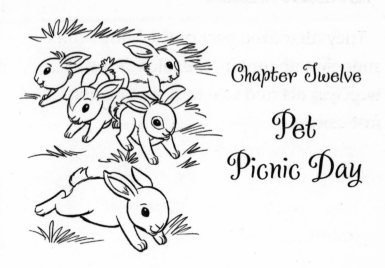

Chapter Twelve

Pet Picnic Day

In the morning, the four princesses got dressed early before the rest of Seahorse Tower was awake and took Daisy down to the pet barn.

Ella kissed the rabbit's floppy ears before placing her back in the hutch with her brothers and sisters. She fetched some extra hay for the rabbits and helped Rebecca move the hay bales into another part of the barn. Daisy hopped up and down her run happily with her ears

 109

pricked up.

"She's still got lots of energy even after hopping down all those passageways," said Lottie, smiling.

"She's quite an adventurous rabbit," said Ella.

"Hey – you know what today is?" said Rosalind, suddenly excited. "It's Pet Picnic Day!"

"Ooh, yes!" said Summer. "I'd forgotten about that."

"What's Pet Picnic Day?" asked Ella.

"Every month we have a picnic and the pets come along too." Rosalind grinned. "And we're allowed to wear our own clothes instead of school uniform."

"And the cooks give us the yummiest cakes and jellies for the picnic," added Summer.

"But the best bit is that each tower takes turns at being in charge and today it's the

turn of Seahorse Tower!" said Lottie.

A shadow fell in the doorway. "Well, you four aren't going to take part in it!" said Molly. "I've told Miss Goldwin that you weren't in your room at bedtime last night. She's coming here right now to tell you off."

Ella's stomach turned over. Then she noticed Molly's mean smile and knew she had to say something. "I'm *really* sorry I knocked you over into the water that time," she said to the older girl. "But it was an accident and I don't think it's fair of you to carry on being angry about it."

"Well said!" Rosalind folded her arms and glared at Molly.

"I know that captains are supposed to make sure people follow the rules," added Ella. "But aren't they also meant to look after new princesses and help them feel at home in Harebell Castle?"

"Yes, Ella," said Miss Goldwin, stepping into the pet barn. "That's *exactly* what they're supposed to do." She gazed at the girls with bright eyes. "As it happens, Rebecca has told me how helpful you've been here in the pet barn. Was there a good reason for you to be out of bed last night?"

"Yes, Miss Goldwin. There was," said Ella truthfully.

The Headmistress turned to the older girl. "You see, Molly. There was no need to worry. But perhaps you'd like to come back to my office where we can talk about your job as a Seahorse Captain."

Molly turned red and muttered, "Yes, Miss Goldwin." Then she left the barn without looking at Ella and the others.

Miss Goldwin smiled. "Now, as it's Pet Picnic Day, you'd better start taking these animals outside. I'm sure the rest of your

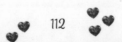

tower will be along soon to help you."

"Yes, Miss Goldwin," said the girls.

The four princesses picked up the rabbits one by one and put them in a run on the grass. Then they rushed inside to get changed into their best dresses ready for the picnic.

Ella put on her beautiful cream-coloured dress decorated with green leaf patterns. She added her favourite bracelets and a tiara with gleaming gold flowers.

Rosalind was wearing a dark-blue dress and a golden tiara that sparkled with sapphires. "I like your bracelets," she told Ella. "They're really pretty."

"Thanks!" Ella smiled.

Lottie pulled on a crimson dress with silk sleeves. Then she squashed a ruby tiara on top of her red curls. "We'd better hurry. We don't want to let the other girls

from our tower do all the work."

"I'm nearly ready!" Summer smoothed her dress, which was edged with red ribbon. Then she quickly brushed her golden hair.

The princesses rushed down to the kitchen where they collected a bundle of picnic blankets and three large baskets. The baskets were filled with sandwiches, sausage rolls and the biggest chocolate cake Ella had ever seen.

They took everything out to the field and began spreading the picnic blankets on the grass. They handed out plates decorated with a starfish pattern and poured glasses of sparkling lemonade for everyone.

The whole school sat down on the picnic blankets to enjoy lunch while their pets played around them. Ella took a bite of delicious chocolate cake. She could see

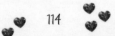

Daisy bouncing up and down, enjoying the fresh air and the warm sunshine.

Lottie's sister, Emily, and her friends from Coral Tower came to sit with Ella and the others. One girl, Freya, was holding a lovely black cat with blue eyes and white paws.

Freya shook back her blonde plaits and said to Lottie, "Do you remember my kitten, Minky? You were staying at my castle in Northernland when Minky got lost in the snow."

"Of course I remember!" said Lottie, stroking the little black cat. "I could never forget you, Minky."

After the picnic, Miss Goldwin organised them into teams ready for a three-legged race and a beanbag race.

Lottie's pony, Strawberry, trotted up to the fence to find out what all the excitement was about. He shook his

long mane and gave a whinny. Then Summer's parrot flew down to perch on her shoulder, not wanting to miss out on the fun either.

Ella picked up Daisy from her rabbit run and hugged her. She looked round at all the girls and their pets having fun together. The castle looked bright in the sunshine. A gentle breeze blew in from the cliffs where the orange-and-white lighthouse gleamed in the middle of a sparkling blue sea.

"Are you all right, Ella?" asked Rosalind.

"I'm so glad I came here," Ella told her with a big smile. "I know I'm going to love being a Rescue Princess."

Look out for these amazing animal adventures at the Rescue Zoo!

Join Pandora and her very special granny for comic chaos and tons of *TROUBLE!*

What would YOU do if your
teacher was an ALIEN?

No real teachers were harmed by aliens
in the making of this book

BABY
ALIENS
GOT MY
TEACHER!

PAMELA
BUTCHART

nosy
crow